SUMMER SCHOOL

Look for these
and other books
in
The Kids in Ms. Colman's Class series

#1 *Teacher's Pet*
#2 *Author Day*
#3 *Class Play*
#4 *Second Grade Baby*
#5 *Snow War*
#6 *Twin Trouble*
#7 *Science Fair*
#8 *Summer School*
#9 *Halloween Parade*

Jannie, Bobby, Tammy, Sara
Ian, Leslie, Hank, Terri
Nancy, Omar, Audrey, Chris, Ms. Colman
Karen, Hannie, Ricky, Natalie

THE KIDS IN MS. COLMAN'S CLASS

SUMMER SCHOOL

Ann M. Martin

Illustrations by Charles Tang

A
LITTLE APPLE
PAPERBACK

SCHOLASTIC INC.
New York Toronto London Auckland Sydney

No part of this publication may be reproduced in whole or in part, or stored in a retrieval system, or transmitted in any form or by any means, electronic, mechanical, photocopying, recording, or otherwise, without written permission of the publisher. For information regarding permission, write to Scholastic Inc., 555 Broadway, New York, NY 10012.

ISBN 0-590-69204-6

Copyright © 1997 by Ann M. Martin. All rights reserved. Published by Scholastic Inc. BABY-SITTER'S LITTLE SISTER and LITTLE APPLE PAPERBACKS are trademarks and/or registered trademarks of Scholastic Inc.

12 11 10 9 8 7 6 5 4 3 2 1   7 8 9/9 0 1 2/0

Printed in the U.S.A.   40

First Scholastic printing, July 1997

*The author gratefully acknowledges
Gabrielle Charbonnet
for her help
with this book.*

SUMMER SCHOOL

Saturday!

That was Audrey Green's first thought when she opened her eyes. This was not just any old Saturday, either. It was the very first Saturday of summer. School was out!

Audrey sat up in bed and felt for Sasha. Sasha was her family's cat. He was very old and very big. For as long as Audrey could remember, Sasha had slept in Audrey's bed with her. Under the covers. Every single night.

Audrey felt around under the sheets. She hauled Sasha up and held him in her arms. Sasha blinked in the sunlight. He yawned. He closed his eyes again.

"Come on," said Audrey. She kissed him between the ears. "Let's go have breakfast."

"Good morning, honey," said Mrs. Green. She put a glass of juice by Audrey's place.

"Morning, Mommy," said Audrey. "Morning, Daddy."

Mr. Green smiled at Audrey over the top of his newspaper. He took another bite of cereal.

"Would you like cereal today or a waffle?" asked Mrs. Green.

"A waffle, please," said Audrey. "I need a special breakfast because it is the first day of summer vacation."

After Mrs. Green had made Audrey's waffle, she sat down. "Are you going to play with Sara today?" she asked.

Audrey nodded and took a bite of her waffle. Sara Ford was in Audrey's second-grade class at Stoneybrook Academy. She lived down the street from Audrey. They were not *best* friends, but they were good friends. Audrey did not have one special best friend. She wished she did, though.

"I spoke to Mrs. Ford yesterday," said Mrs. Green. "It is too bad that Sara will not be going to the Stoneybrook Academy day camp. Mrs. Ford said they will be too busy to sign up for a two-week session. I am sorry. I know it would be fun for you if Sara went, too."

Audrey frowned. "I do not want to go to summer school," she said. "I like school, and I like Ms. Colman, but summertime is for playing."

Mr. Green put down his newspaper. "It is not summer school, Audrey," he said. "It is *day camp*. Day camp will not be like school. It will be more fun. You will play games and do arts and crafts. You will read books and play sports and do all sorts of fun things."

"I still do not want to go," said Audrey.

"You will know everyone there," said Mrs. Green. "There will be nine kids from Ms. Colman's class, and six kids from Mr. Berger's class. They are all your friends."

Mr. Berger taught the other second-grade class at Stoneybrook Academy.

"And Ms. Colman will be in charge of your day-camp group," added Mr. Green.

"I just want to stay at home," said Audrey. "I want to play all day. I want to watch daytime TV."

"Audrey. You may not watch daytime TV even if you do stay home all day," said Mrs. Green. "Anyway, your father and I both work. There is no one here to look after you."

"Could Allen come home and look after me?" asked Audrey in a small voice. Allen was her older brother. He was nice, but he was eleven years older than she was. He had been away at college for two years and came home only for holidays. Sometimes Audrey felt as if she hardly

5

knew him. But even Allen would be better than day camp.

Mrs. Green sighed. "Allen is doing a work-study program this summer, honey. He will be home only for one week at the end of August. He cannot come home to take care of you."

"Day camp will be fun," said Mr. Green firmly. "Each two-week session has a theme. This first session is Book Camp. You will all be reading fun books. You like to read. You are a good reader."

"And the session after that is Theater Camp," said Mrs. Green. "You will write plays and act them out. You will make costumes. Each day-camp session will have a new, fun, different theme. You will see. I know you will have a good time."

Audrey was not so sure. But she could tell that her parents did not want to talk about it anymore. She finished her waffle. She did not want to talk about it anymore either.

2

SARA

"No, no, the flower girl goes first," said Sara Ford. She walked her baby doll down a pretend aisle. Audrey and Sara were playing wedding at Sara's house.

"Could Frederick be the flower dog?" asked Audrey. Frederick was Sara's new dachshund puppy. Audrey thought he was so, so cute.

"We could try," said Sara. She looked around for Frederick.

So far, the first Saturday of summer vacation was going okay, Audrey decided. After breakfast that morning, she and her parents had gone to the mall. Mrs. Green had bought Audrey some new shorts and

T-shirts for day camp. Audrey had also gotten a new pair of sandals. They were white with pink and purple butterflies sewn onto the straps. They were great.

The Greens had eaten lunch at the food court. Audrey had ordered a combination Chinese-food plate. Eating lunch out was fun.

And now Audrey was at Sara's house. Playing wedding was one of their favorite games.

Sara came back in, holding Frederick around his middle. He drooped down at both ends, because he was so long.

The girls brushed his short black hair until it was shiny. They tied some scarves and some plastic flowers to his collar. He made an excellent flower dog.

"I wish you were coming to day camp with me," said Audrey.

"Me too," said Sara. "But my parents and I will be taking little trips all summer long. So I cannot go. You will have fun, though."

"Maybe," said Audrey. "I do not want to go to Stoneybrook Academy every day, like I do all year. It will not feel like summertime."

"I bet it will feel very different," said Sara. "Like it does on Parents Night or something. Like school, but more fun."

"I guess. Anyway, let's start again," said Audrey. "This time I will be the bride."

Audrey fastened a white towel to her headband. "Dum, *dum*, da-*dum*," she hummed. The towel flowed down her back like a real bridal veil. Audrey took off her new sandals and put on a pair of Mrs. Ford's high heels.

Sara waited for her at the wedding altar (which was really Sara's bedside table).

Frederick trotted down the aisle. Then he flopped down beside the altar and fell asleep with his paws in the air.

Audrey giggled. She wobbled on her high heels and tripped on her veil. "Oh!" she cried. She fell forward, her hands outstretched, and landed on Frederick. He yelped and scrambled away, knocking over the altar. It crashed to the floor. Frederick got tangled in the scarves and paddled his short legs. He yelped again.

Sara was laughing so hard, she could hardly stand up.

"Wait, Freddie!" she cried. She managed to grab Frederick long enough to untangle him. As soon as he was free, he dashed out of the room.

Audrey stood up. Her veil had come off. Her shoes had been kicked across the room. She and Sara picked up the bedside table.

Audrey felt embarrassed. "I am sorry. I did not mean to trip. I hope I did not hurt Frederick."

"Oh, he is fine," said Sara, still giggling. "It was so funny. You are not hurt, are you?"

Audrey shook her head. She finished cleaning up the mess. "Things like this always happen to me," she said. "I guess I am just clumsy. Remember when I threw that iceball and accidentally knocked Ian's tooth out?" That had been last winter.

Sara nodded, and giggled again. "And the time you were holding Bobby's mouse and she accidentally got away. Bobby could not finish his science project."

Audrey shrugged. "I did not mean to."

"Do not worry about it," said Sara. "It is not a big deal. Now, do you want to play Cootie, or Junior Scrabble, or Junior Pictionary?"

Audrey thought. "Junior Pictionary." She smiled as Sara went to get the game. Sara was a good friend. The summer would be perfect if only Sara could go to day camp, too.

THE FIRST DAY

On Monday morning Audrey lay around in her bed. It was the first day of day camp. Mrs. Green came into Audrey's room and opened her curtains.

"Rise and shine," she said cheerfully.

Audrey groaned quietly. She still did not want to go to day camp.

Mrs. Green smiled at her. "Sweet rolls for breakfast," she said, and left the room.

Audrey fished Sasha up from under the covers. "I wish you could come with me," she whispered into Sasha's fur. Then she rolled out of bed.

* * *

Mrs. Green dropped Audrey off in front of Stoneybrook Academy. Audrey wore a small backpack. Inside it was her swimsuit, a towel, a spare T-shirt, and her lunch.

"Have a wonderful day," said Mrs. Green.

"A wonderful day at summer school?" asked Audrey sadly. "I do not think so." Then she climbed out of the car and walked to the playground.

Audrey's second-grade teacher, Ms. Colman, was on the playground. So were many kids from Ms. Colman's class. Karen Brewer was sitting on a seesaw with one of her best friends, Nancy Dawes. Tammy and Terri Barkan, the twins, were playing hopscotch with Michelle Rivers, from Mr. Berger's class. Omar Harris, Ian Johnson, and Hank Reubens were playing foursquare with Michael Davidson, also from Mr. Berger's class. Jannie Gilbert was jumping rope with Debbie Dvorak and

Nina Bluesky, two more girls from Mr. Berger's class.

Audrey sighed. She liked everyone here. They were all her friends. But she did not have a best friend.

Soon a bell rang.

Just like in school, thought Audrey.

Ms. Colman clapped her hands. "All second-graders, come with me, please," she called.

This is different, thought Audrey. Usually when the bell rang, everyone lined up and marched to his or her classroom. But now Ms. Colman was leading the campers to the gym.

Inside the gym, groups of kids were sitting on the floor. Each group was a grade. A teacher was in charge of each grade. And several teenagers were helping out, too. Ms. Colman led her group to an open space. She asked them to sit in a circle.

Audrey sat between Karen Brewer and Debbie Dvorak.

"Good morning, campers," said Ms.

Colman. "You all know me, of course. I would like to introduce you to Susan Perez and Tom Baldwin. They will be our assistant camp counselors."

An older girl, with brown shoulder-length hair, smiled at the group. She looked nice, Audrey decided. The boy looked nice, too. He had shiny black hair and soft brown eyes. Susan and Tom seemed friendly. Audrey felt a little better.

"Before we return to the playground," said Ms. Colman, "I would like to explain the camp program. Each morning we will meet on the playground. When the bell rings, come to the gym and find your group. The whole camp will sing some good-morning songs, just to wake us up and get us into the camp spirit. Then we will join other campers on the playground for sports and outdoor games."

Karen raised her hand. Karen was kind of bossy, but Audrey liked her. Maybe Karen could be Audrey's special camp friend.

"Yes, Karen?" said Ms. Colman.

"Will we do arts and crafts?" asked Karen.

"Yes," answered Ms. Colman. "Our schedule will change each day, but we will have time for sing-alongs, drama classes, free periods, arts and crafts, and water fun. We will also have guest teachers who will share interesting topics with us. And this Friday we will take a surprise field trip."

"If we know we are going," said Ian, "it will not be a surprise."

Ms. Colman smiled. "But *do* you know where we are going?"

"No," admitted Ian.

"I love surprises," whispered Karen. Audrey could feel Karen wiggle a bit with excitement.

"Are there any questions?" asked Ms. Colman.

No one had any questions. Ms. Colman was a very good explainer.

"Okay, then," said Ms. Colman. "Let's join our fellow campers at the front of the

17

gym for some good-morning songs."

Karen jumped up and ran to the front of the gym. She did not wait for Audrey. Who would Audrey's special camp friend be? Maybe Tammy and Terri? Or how about Jannie Gilbert? Jannie's best friend, Leslie Morris, was not here.

"Come on! Let's sit together," said a voice.

Audrey turned around. There was Debbie Dvorak, from Mr. Berger's class. Audrey did not know Debbie very well. Debbie smiled and pointed to the front of the gym. "Come on," she repeated, giving Audrey's arm a little tug.

Audrey smiled at Debbie. Debbie had thick, straight, light blonde hair and brown eyes. She looked nice.

"Okay," said Audrey.

Audrey and Debbie sat down together at the front of the gym. The very first morning of day camp had just started. And Audrey had already made a new friend.

Book Camp

All morning Debbie and Audrey stayed together. When they played capture the flag with the first-graders, Debbie made sure she and Audrey were on the same team.

After capture the flag, they played kickball with the third-graders. Audrey kicked the ball as hard as she could, then ran to first base.

"Go, Audrey, go!" yelled Debbie.

Audrey smiled as she ran. It felt good to have someone rooting for her.

At lunchtime Audrey and Debbie sat together under the big oak tree in the playground. Because this was day camp, they had a choice. They could sit inside at tables in the cafeteria. Or they could sit outside anywhere they wanted. Like a picnic.

Sara had been right, Audrey thought. Day camp *was* different from going to school every day. Audrey was at school, but she was not doing the usual school things. Playing games and having different rules almost made Audrey feel like she was on vacation. And there was no math or science or social studies or spelling. That helped.

As lunch was ending, Ms. Colman gathered the second-graders into a group again. They sat on the cool cement under the cafeteria overhang. Audrey sipped from a juice can, then set it down next to her.

"As you know," said Ms. Colman, "this first two-week session is Book Camp. That means we will focus on books and reading. You will each choose one book to read. After you finish it, you will create a project about that book. The project may be anything you wish. You could act out a scene from the story or draw a picture. You could even make a costume and tell the story as one of the characters in the book. On the last day of camp, you will present your project. We will have a special program to which you may invite family members."

"Cool!" said Karen. (She had not raised her hand.) "Can we choose any book we want?"

"Yes," said Ms. Colman. "Right now we will go to the school library. You will have half an hour to choose a book. Please let me know if you need any help."

Everyone stood up to go to the library. Audrey forgot about the can of juice next to her. Her foot knocked it over, and it spilled onto the cement.

"Oops," said Audrey. She quickly picked up the can.

"That is okay," said Ms. Colman. "But please clean it up so that we do not have any ants. Meet us in the library when you are done."

"I will stay and help Audrey," said Debbie.

Debbie and Audrey mopped up the juice with paper towels. Then Audrey filled her juice can with water and dumped it on the sticky cement.

"Thank you for helping," she said.

"No problem," answered Debbie. "What are friends for?"

"Have you found one yet?" whispered Debbie.

Audrey jumped. She was sitting on the floor of the library, between two rows of books. After looking and looking, she had finally found a book for her project. It was called *Sarah, Plain and Tall*, by Patricia MacLachlan. She had already started reading it.

"Yes," answered Audrey. She showed Debbie the cover. "What did you pick?"

Debbie held up her book. It was called *The Mystery of Lilac Inn*. "It is about two sisters who are detectives," said Debbie.

23

"Cool," said Audrey. "What will you do for your project?"

"I do not know yet," said Debbie. "I will decide after I read the book."

After all the kids had chosen books, they went back outside. They sat under the large oak tree and read their books. Ms. Colman and the two counselors, Tom and Susan, were there to help with difficult words.

Audrey liked her book. She was on page nine when Ms. Colman announced that it was time for water fun. Audrey looked at Debbie and smiled. Water fun! Day camp was feeling less like summer school all the time.

5

AUDREY'S SHADOW

On Tuesday morning Debbie was waiting for Audrey at the edge of the playground. She waved and smiled when Audrey got out of her mother's car.

" 'Bye, Mommy," said Audrey.

" 'Bye, honey," said Mrs. Green. "Have a good day."

"Hi, Audrey!" called Debbie. "Look, I saved the seesaw for us. I left my backpack on one of the seats. Come on."

"Hey, Audrey," said Tammy. She and Terri were about to start a game of hopscotch. "Want to play?"

"Um," said Audrey. Hopscotch did sound like fun.

"First we are going to seesaw," said Debbie. Gently she tugged Audrey's arm.

Audrey looked back at Tammy and shrugged. "Maybe later," she called. She did not really want to ride the seesaw. But it had been nice of Debbie to save it for her.

Audrey found that Tuesday was even more fun than Monday. In the morning the kids sang camp songs and played sports. Then Susan, their counselor, had led the second-graders in a very silly game of follow the leader. They had had to climb the monkey bars, then hop across the playground on one foot, then walk backward while singing "John Jacob Jingleheimer Schmidt." By the end of the game, Audrey was laughing so hard she could hardly sing.

Then they had eaten lunch. This time Audrey did not spill her juice.

After lunch, they had quiet period. The campers read their books under the oak tree. All morning long Debbie had stuck to Audrey's side like taffy. Whenever they played a game that needed partners, Debbie was there. They had eaten lunch together. Now Debbie was reading her book next to Audrey.

Audrey was glad to have a special camp friend. But she liked everyone else in her group, too. Sometimes Audrey wanted to play with some of the other campers. But Debbie always seemed to get between them. Audrey guessed that Debbie needed a friend. It would not hurt Audrey to try to be a good friend to her.

"All right, campers," said Ms. Colman. "Quiet period is over for today. Now it is time for drama. We are going to start by playing a fun game."

"Oh, goody," said Karen. "I love drama."

"Goody gumdrops," said Terri.

"The game is called charades," said Ms. Colman. "You will pick a slip of paper out of this hat." She held up a straw hat. "The paper will list the title of a movie or a book. You will then have to act out that title. We, the audience, will try to guess what it is. The audience may also ask yes-or-no questions. You can respond by shaking or nodding your head. But the person acting out the title may not say a single word."

Audrey grinned. Charades sounded like fun. She hoped she would draw an easy title. She also hoped that someone else would go first. That way she could see how it was done.

"Tom has volunteered to go first," said Ms. Colman. "Then you will understand how to play."

Good old Ms. Colman, thought Audrey. She always thinks of everything.

"And then it was my turn. I picked *Beauty and the Beast*," Audrey reported at dinner that night.

"How did you act it out?" asked Mrs. Green.

"First I walked around, acting fancy and beautiful. Then I hunched over and made my hands into claws and showed my teeth. Like this." Audrey grimaced at her parents and bared her teeth.

"Ooh. Very beastlike," said Mr. Green.

"Ms. Colman said I did a very good job," said Audrey.

"Good for you, honey," said Mrs. Green. "So was it a little bit fun, then?"

"Yeah," said Audrey. "Summer school

is not *too* bad, I guess. But Debbie Dvorak is there every time I turn around. She is nice. But she is *always there*."

"Maybe she will make more friends as day camp goes on," said Mrs. Green.

"I hope so," said Audrey.

ARTS AND CRAFTS

By Thursday, Audrey had finished reading her book. Now it was time to come up with a project about it. She decided she would ask Ms. Colman for help after lunch.

That morning they sang camp songs, as usual. Audrey liked "Good Morning to You" and "Here We Go A-Camping." They were cheerful songs. Then, since it was a very hot day, the counselors decided to have water fun first instead of team sports. Everyone scrambled to change into his or her swimsuit.

"I want Audrey on my team," said Jannie, once they were all gathered outside. Audrey smiled and stood by Jannie.

"No fair," said Debbie. "Audrey and I have to be on the same team." Debbie had already been chosen for Ian's team.

"I think you can be on different teams just this once," said Ms. Colman. "Now, both teams need to get ready."

Audrey could not believe what happened next. A water-balloon war. At *school*

Each team was given a large bucket of water balloons. The kids chased each other around, throwing the balloons. There were a few rules: Campers had to stay in the playing field and not go on the cement. There was to be no throwing at anyone's head. And no ganging up on anyone.

Audrey had never, ever expected to have so much fun at day camp. And it was nice not to have Debbie by her side the whole time.

Finally Ms. Colman clapped her hands. "Time to dry off and have lunch," she called.

"Rats," said Audrey.

After lunch and quiet period, it was

time for arts and crafts. Audrey talked to Ms. Colman about her project. Audrey decided to draw pictures for *Sarah, Plain and Tall*, since there were no pictures in the book. (Audrey had felt very grown-up, reading a book with no pictures in it.)

For arts and crafts Audrey's group met in Ms. Colman's classroom. Audrey felt strange being in her classroom in the summertime. Day camp was held mostly outside, and sometimes in the gym and cafeteria.

Hootie, the class guinea pig, was not there. He was taking turns staying with Audrey's classmates over the summer. (It would be Audrey's turn at the end of July. Audrey wondered how Hootie and Sasha would get along.) The classroom seemed empty without Hootie.

"Where do you usually sit?" asked Debbie. "I want to sit by you."

Audrey sighed to herself. "I sit there," she said. "What are you going to do for your project?"

"Well," said Debbie. "In my mystery book, the final clue was found in a clock. So I am going to make a clock out of a cardboard box. Then I will put the clue inside. The clue is a secret. People will have to guess the secret. Then I will open the clock and show them."

"Cool," said Audrey. "That is a very good project."

Debbie blushed and looked pleased. "Thank you. That is why I like you, Audrey. You are very nice." Debbie ran off to get some arts-and-crafts materials.

Audrey thought about what Debbie had said. I am nice, but I am not *amazingly* nice. Maybe Debbie is not used to nice people. Maybe that is why she wants to be with me all the time.

Audrey decided to use colored pencils for her pictures. She found several sheets of paper and a large coffee can full of colored pencils. She sat down at her desk next to Debbie. Then she began to draw.

First she drew a picture of Anna and

Caleb, the two children in the book. She drew sad faces on them. They were sad because they had no mother.

"Ms. Colman!" called Jannie. "Is it supposed to look like this?" Jannie held up a brush. There was goo dripping off it. Jannie was making something out of papier-mâché.

Audrey looked up to see what Jannie was talking about. Then she reached for a yellow pencil. She did not notice that the can of colored pencils was on the very edge of her desk. Audrey knocked the can to the floor.

Crash! The metal made a loud noise. Colored pencils scattered everywhere, across the floor and under the desks.

"Oh my goodness!" cried Debbie. "That was not your fault, Audrey. Your desk is wobbly."

Audrey frowned as she picked up the pencils. Her desk was not wobbly. She had simply knocked the can over. Debbie was making a big deal out of it.

Debbie stooped down to help Audrey pick up the pencils. "This can is not good for holding pencils," she said. "It falls too easily. We should use something else. I will tell Ms. Colman."

"No, do not worry about it," said Audrey. Her voice sounded a tiny bit angry. Why did Debbie have to help her? Now everyone was looking at Audrey. She felt embarrassed.

Finally Audrey picked up the last pencil. She put the can in the middle of her desk. She would try very hard not to knock it over again.

Debbie began to paint her clock brown. Audrey did not even look at her.

7

AUDREY'S PROBLEM

"Mommy, can Sara come over?" asked Audrey when she got home.

"I do not see why not," said Mrs. Green.

Audrey and Sara shared a snack. They drank juice and ate grapes and rice cakes with peanut butter. Then they played jacks on the front porch.

"So what did you do today?" Audrey asked Sara.

"I went grocery shopping with Mommy. Then we got new shoes for Marcus." Marcus was Sara's older brother. "What did you do?"

Audrey told Sara about the water-balloon war, and about having lunch outside like a picnic, and about arts and crafts and sing-along time.

"That sounds great," said Sara. "You are having so much fun."

"Yes," said Audrey. She finished three-sies and threw the jacks again. "Except . . . do you remember Debbie Dvorak, from Mr. Berger's class?"

"Uh-huh. Oops, you missed. My turn." Sara took the jacks and the ball.

"Debbie is at day camp too," said Audrey. "She follows me everywhere. Debbie is nice, but she never leaves me alone."

"Hmm. Does she have a best friend?" asked Sara.

"No. She is friends with everyone. But I think she has decided that I am her best friend. She is like my Siamese twin."

The girls giggled.

"Every time I have an accident, Debbie

rushes to help me," said Audrey. "I wish she would not do that. It just makes things worse."

Sara nodded. "I bet Debbie wants a best friend," she said. "Maybe she is lonely. Maybe that is why she is being a pain."

"I guess," said Audrey. "I do not mind being friends with her. She is very nice. But she is *too much*."

After jacks, Audrey and Sara decided to swing in Audrey's backyard. They walked around the side of the house.

"Have I told you about my camp project?" asked Audrey.

"No. What are you doing?" said Sara.

"I am drawing — *oh!*" Audrey had stepped on the end of a garden rake. The rake snapped up and hit her shoulder. Audrey pushed it away, and the rake fell against a stack of clay flower pots. Several pots broke.

Audrey and Sara stared at the broken pots. Then Sara's eyes met Audrey's. The corners of Sara's mouth turned up. She started giggling, her hand over her mouth. Her giggle turned into a laugh. Soon both Audrey and Sara were laughing very hard.

"You did it again!" cried Sara.

Audrey laughed and nodded.

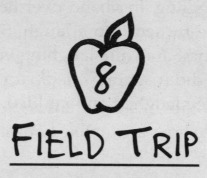

FIELD TRIP

On Friday morning Ms. Colman gathered her group together.

"Today is our surprise field trip," she reminded them. "Here is our school bus."

"Please choose a partner, everyone," said Susan, the counselor.

Debbie grabbed Audrey's hand. "We will be partners," she cried.

Audrey wished Jannie Gilbert was her partner. Jannie would have made a nice change. Jannie and Nina Bluesky decided to be partners. Audrey sighed.

"Where are we going, Ms. Colman?" asked Omar Harris.

"Here is a clue," said Ms. Colman.

"This is *Book* Camp. Our field trip has to do with our theme."

"A bookstore?" called Karen.

"No. We are going to see how books are printed," said Ms. Colman. "There is a printing company about half an hour away. We will see how they make books."

"Cool," said Karen.

"This will be neat," said Audrey. "I have never seen a book being made."

The printing company was called TMJ Repro.

"It looks like an office building," said Hank as the bus pulled up in front of TMJ Repro.

Inside, a woman greeted them. Her name badge said CAROLINE JACOBS.

"Hello, and welcome to TMJ," she said. "I understand you have been doing a lot of reading lately."

"We have been going to Book Camp," said Karen.

"Well, you are in luck today. We are printing a new picture book," said Ms.

Jacobs. "Come with me, and I will show you."

Ms. Colman's group passed through a large room full of desks and computers. Ms. Jacobs explained that designers and artists worked at them.

Then Ms. Jacobs pushed through some swinging doors. Audrey's eyes widened. She was standing in a huge room full of enormous machines. The machines were whirring and clicking and swishing. A yucky chemical smell was in the

air. Audrey wrinkled her nose.

"Ugh," said Debbie. "It smells terrible in here."

Ms. Jacobs overheard her. "You're smelling the ink from the presses. I guess I am used to it." She walked closer to a machine that practically reached the ceiling. On it were big metal rollers that were spinning fast. Audrey could see them sucking up large sheets of paper, as big as her bed at home. The paper whirled around several metal rollers. Then the machine spit it out

on the other side. When it came out, it was printed with words and pictures.

Several kids stepped closer to the machine. Audrey tried to join them, but Debbie held her back.

"I do not want to go closer," said Debbie. "That machine is scary."

Audrey rolled her eyes.

Ms. Jacobs lifted one of the big sheets of paper from the stack. It smelled new and crisp and hot. There were sixteen different pictures printed on it. They were all out of order. Some of them were upside down. Ms. Jacobs explained that the sheet would be folded up and cut into book-size pages. It would be the inside of a picture book. Audrey thought that was neat.

With Debbie hanging on to her hand, Audrey toured the rest of the printing plant. Ms. Colman's group saw how the insides of books are glued, sewn, or stapled into their covers. They saw how the large sheets of paper were printed with four different colors — black, blue, red, and yellow. The kids saw how every picture in a book is made of thousands of tiny, tiny dots of ink. It was hard to believe, but it was true.

Afterward Ms. Colman's group thanked Ms. Jacobs for the tour. They climbed back into their school bus.

"That was gigundoly cool," said Karen. "I loved seeing how a book is made."

"Yes," said Audrey. "I will think of that tour every time I read a new book."

"Those machines were kind of scary," said Debbie. "I was worried you would trip and fall into them, Audrey. I did not want you to get smushed."

Audrey stared at Debbie. "I am not a baby, Debbie," she said. She felt angry. "You do not have to protect me."

"I am sorry," said Debbie. "Please do not be angry at me. I just did not want you to be hurt, because I like you so much."

Audrey looked out the window. She did not say anything.

THE GIANT
PEACH DISASTER

By Wednesday of the next week, Audrey was no longer angry at Debbie. They played together. They ate lunch together. And they sat by each other during arts and crafts.

During arts and crafts each day, Audrey worked on her book project. She had completed six drawings for *Sarah, Plain and Tall*. Some of her drawings were better than others. But on the whole she liked them.

Debbie had finished her clock on Tuesday. On Wednesday she brought in an old-fashioned key. She showed it to Audrey.

Then she hid it inside the clock when no one was looking. She taped the clock shut.

Karen and Nancy were doing a project together. Karen had written a skit based on a book called *Tutu Much Ballet*, by Gabrielle Charbonnet. The book was about a girl who did not want to take ballet lessons. Karen and Nancy were acting out a chapter from it.

Hank had read about Robin Hood and his Merry Men. He was making a Robin Hood costume. Tom Baldwin was helping him with the bow and arrow.

Jannie had read *James and the Giant Peach*, by Roald Dahl. She was making a huge papier-mâché peach. It was almost finished. It was bigger than a basketball. She had painted it to look like a peach. She was going to add some paper leaves to the stem.

"That peach looks like a big belly button," said Hank.

"Oh, be quiet, Hank," said Jannie.

All the campers were finishing up

their projects. Some kids were going to recite poems. Some were going to perform skits. A couple of kids were going to show illustrations for their books, like Audrey.

The day passed. Soon most of the campers had left. Audrey's mother was going to pick her up in just a few minutes. Audrey stacked her pictures neatly in her day-camp cubby. Debbie waited for her. They were alone in the room.

"There. I have only one more picture to do," said Audrey. "I will be ready on Friday."

"Good," said Debbie. "You have worked very hard on your project."

Audrey took a step back. And somehow . . . she lost her balance. She fell backward, swinging her arms like a windmill.

"Oh!" she cried, crashing into a desk. Jannie's humongous peach was on the desk. The peach fell to the floor. And Audrey fell on top of it.

It was very quiet in the classroom. Audrey could feel the peach under her. She

had crushed it completely. She looked at Debbie. Debbie's hands were on her cheeks.

Slowly Audrey got up. Debbie straightened the desk. "Are you all right?" she asked.

"Yes. But look at Jannie's peach," said Audrey miserably. Audrey picked up the peach and set it on the desk. It was a big, hollow, smushed mess. Audrey thought of how hard Jannie had worked on it. She leaned against the cubbies and held her head in her hands. This was terrible. What should she do?

"Goodness!" said Ms. Colman, standing in the doorway. "What happened here?"

"Well, I — " began Audrey.

"We do not know," interrupted Debbie. "We came in to put our projects away, and we found Jannie's peach like this."

Audrey stared at Debbie. Debbie was lying to Ms. Colman. Audrey knew she should tell the truth. She did not want to. But she had to.

"You see, I — " Audrey began again.

"Someone must have come in here before us," said Debbie. "It is too bad about Jannie's peach. But we do not know what happened. We *swear*."

"Hmm. I see. Very well, girls," said Ms. Colman. "You may go. I will get to the bottom of this somehow."

"Come on, Audrey," said Debbie. Debbie grabbed Audrey's backpack and pulled her out of the room.

Audrey followed her. She was very confused.

THE PEACH PROBLEM

Just as Audrey and Debbie were leaving the room, Jannie ran in.

"I forgot my backpack," she said. She grabbed it out of her cubby. She was about to run back out when she saw the peach.

Her mouth opened in a big O. She stared at the peach.

She gasped. "Wha — what happened?"

"I do not know," said Ms. Colman. "Debbie says she and Audrey found the peach like this a few minutes ago."

"Oh," said Jannie. "It is ruined. I have been working on it for a week! I will never be able to make another peach by Friday."

Audrey felt terrible.

Jannie started to cry. Then she pushed her peach to the floor. Ms. Colman knelt next to her and patted her back.

"I am very sorry," said Ms. Colman. "I know how hard you worked on your peach. We will try to find out what happened to it."

Jannie just cried.

In front of school, Audrey and Debbie sat down to wait for their mothers. Mrs. Green was not usually late.

Hurry up, Mommy, thought Audrey.

"Whew!" said Debbie cheerfully. "That was close. I got you out of a big mess, huh?"

"Debbie, you lied to Ms. Colman," said Audrey. "Lying is wrong. We should have told the truth."

"Are you crazy?" squealed Debbie. "You would have gotten in so much trouble! And Jannie would have hated you forever."

"It was an accident," said Audrey. "I would have apologized. Maybe Jannie would have forgiven me after awhile. But we should not have lied."

"You do not *want* to be in trouble, do you?" said Debbie. "Anyway, it is too late now. Here is my mother." She ran across the yard and jumped into her mother's car.

Audrey put her chin in her hands. She did not know what to think.

That afternoon Audrey played at Sara's house. Marcus kicked them out of the family room, so they went to Sara's bedroom. Audrey did not feel much like playing. She sat on the floor and rubbed Frederick behind his ears. One of his hind legs kicked the air.

Audrey told Sara the whole sad story. "Jannie's peach was humongous and beautiful. And I ruined it," she said. "Now Jannie will have nothing to show on Family Day. I feel awful. But I feel even worse that Debbie lied for me."

"Debbie should not have done that," agreed Sara. "I think you should tell Ms. Colman the truth."

"I know," said Audrey. "I will. But I am not looking forward to it. It is going to be horrible."

THE MYSTERY OF THE CRUSHED PEACH

On Thursday morning Ms. Colman called a meeting of her campers.

She opened a large shopping bag. She took out what was left of Jannie's peach.

"This was Jannie's book project," said Ms. Colman. "Somehow it has gotten crushed."

A couple of kids said, "Oh, no."

"I need to know who did this," said Ms. Colman. "Jannie and I are both very upset. I am sure it was an accident. The person who did it will not be in trouble, *if* he or she comes to me and explains."

61

"I bet it was Audrey," said Hank. "She is always knocking things over and breaking things."

Everyone turned to look at Audrey. She felt her face flush pink. She decided to tell everyone the truth right then.

"It was *not* Audrey," cried Debbie. "I was there the whole time. We *found* the peach like that. For once it was not Audrey. She really did not do it. I promise." Debbie crossed her heart with her finger.

Audrey glared at Debbie. What could she say now? If she told the truth, she and Debbie would *both* be in trouble. Audrey was starting to think that Debbie's lie was worse than breaking the peach in the first place.

Ms. Colman put the peach back in the shopping bag. She frowned. "I hope someone tells me the truth," she said.

Then she led the group to the playground, for team games with the firstgraders.

Audrey's stomach hurt.

FAMILY DAY

"I thought this day would never come," said Audrey.

"I know," said Terri. Audrey and Terri were walking to the playground. "The last day of Book Camp. Is your project ready?"

"Yes," said Audrey.

"Hi, Audrey!" called Debbie. "I'm over here!" Debbie was swinging on a swing. Audrey sighed and headed over to her.

Jannie was sitting under the oak tree by herself. She looked very sad. Audrey felt terrible all over again.

"You know what?" said Debbie as she and Audrey swung side by side. "I heard Terri and Tammy say they are not coming

64

to camp next session. On Monday, when Theater Camp starts, I bet there will be some new kids. That will be fun."

Good, thought Audrey. Maybe one of them will be your new best friend.

The morning was like every other morning at day camp. But the afternoon was different. Right after lunch, Family Day began. Audrey felt excited about it. Mr. and Mrs. Green were taking the afternoon off from work to come to Family Day. Audrey could not wait to show them her book project.

Audrey's group was going to share their presentations in Ms. Colman's classroom. Audrey and the other campers had made special decorations for the room. It looked very festive. Ms. Colman had brought cupcakes and punch for the guests. Soon the parents began to arrive.

"Mommy!" said Audrey when she saw Mrs. Green. Mr. Green arrived soon afterward. Audrey served them cupcakes and punch. Then she showed them the class's decorations.

"Has it been a terrible two weeks for you?" asked Mrs. Green.

"There have been ups and downs," said Audrey. "But mostly ups."

Across the room Audrey saw Jannie sitting with her parents. Jannie still looked glum. Audrey swallowed hard.

Ms. Colman clapped her hands for attention. "I would like to thank our guests for coming today," she said. "Our campers have been working hard on their Book Camp presentations. Karen, would you and Nancy like to begin our program?"

"Yes!" cried Karen. She and Nancy jumped up. They ran to the coatroom to put on their costumes. Soon they came back and acted a short scene from Karen's book. The girl who did not want to go to ballet class was very funny.

Next Ian read a new ending he had written for his book. "I did not like the ending in the book," he explained. "It was too sad. I like my happy ending better."

Audrey went next. She told the story of *Sarah, Plain and Tall.* Then she held up her drawings and explained them. Her parents clapped loudly. Audrey felt very proud.

Nina Bluesky had written a song about her book. She sang it to the audience. Audrey thought that took a lot of guts.

Hank's Robin Hood costume was a big success.

Michelle Rivers read a poem.

Then Ms. Colman said gently, "Jannie? Would you like to explain about your project?"

Jannie walked to the front of the room. She was holding a large shopping bag. "I read the book *James and the Giant Peach*, by Roald Dahl," she said. "He is an English writer. Then I made this big papier-mâché peach."

Jannie pulled the ruined peach out of the bag, and Audrey felt her face go red. A couple of kids snickered.

When Jannie heard them, she dropped the peach back into the bag and burst into tears. Then she ran out of the room.

Audrey sank down in her chair. She could not stand seeing Jannie so unhappy, when it was all her fault. She knew what she had to do.

13

TO TELL THE TRUTH

After the last presentation, all of the parents and guests clapped. The campers stood in a line at the front of the room and took a bow. Then everyone left to go to the gym, where the entire camp would sing songs.

"Go ahead, Mommy and Daddy," said Audrey. "I need to talk to Ms. Colman for a minute. Okay?"

"Okay," said Mrs. Green.

When Audrey was alone with Ms. Colman, she took a deep breath.

"I am not sure how it happened," she began nervously. "But I broke Jannie's peach. It was an accident. I tripped, and then — smush."

"I see," said Ms. Colman.

"I was going to tell you right away, as soon as you came in," said Audrey. "But then . . . things happened. I did not know what to do." She did not say that Debbie had lied. She did not want to tattle on Debbie.

"I *wanted* to tell the truth," said Audrey. "I know lying is wrong. And I wanted to apologize to Jannie. I feel terrible about her peach."

"I see," said Ms. Colman again. "I am very glad you have told me this, Audrey. It was brave of you to tell me the truth. I think we need to find Jannie, don't you?"

"Yes," said Audrey.

Jannie was not as upset as Audrey had thought she would be.

"I am so, so, so, so sorry, Jannie," said Audrey. "You worked hard on your peach. I felt awful when I broke it. I should have told you right away. I am very sorry."

"It is okay, I guess," said Jannie. "I know it was an accident, since it was you. You would not do it on purpose."

"No, I would not," agreed Audrey. "Do you forgive me?"

"Well, yes," said Jannie.

Ms. Colman thanked the girls. Then she told Audrey she would like to speak to her parents in private. After that, she wanted to speak to Debbie.

Audrey felt *much* better.

DEBBIE IS ANGRY

Soon Family Day was over. Mr. and Mrs. Green were proud of Audrey for telling the truth. They thought she should have told it sooner, though.

Audrey agreed.

Audrey had not seen Debbie since she had apologized to Jannie. Jannie had told Karen about it. Then blabbermouth Karen had told everyone else. And Ms. Colman had asked to speak to Debbie alone.

Audrey found Debbie bouncing a ball against the wall of the cafeteria. "Hi," said Audrey.

Debbie ignored her. Bounce, bounce, bounce.

"Your clock worked out great," said Audrey.

Bounce.

"Are you angry with me?" asked Audrey.

"Yes," said Debbie. "You tattled to Ms. Colman. You got us both in trouble."

"I only tattled on *me*," said Audrey. "I did not even mention you to Ms. Colman."

"Still," said Debbie. "She knew I had lied. Now I have to write one page explaining why lying is wrong."

"Lying *is* wrong," said Audrey.

"I was trying to help you, because I am your friend!"

"I know," said Audrey. "But you were helping in the wrong way. A real friend would have helped me tell the truth."

Debbie glared at her. "Oh! So now I am not a *real* friend! Well, guess what, Miss Stuck-up Audrey. I will not be coming to the next day-camp session. So you will have plenty of time to find a *real* friend!"

"That is not what I meant," said Audrey.

"Oh, never mind," snapped Debbie. "I do not want to talk to you anymore." She turned and ran away, leaving Audrey looking after her.

15

A REAL FRIEND

"I am glad you told the truth," said Sara. After day camp, Sara had come over to Audrey's house. Audrey and Sara were soaking up the air-conditioning in Audrey's family room.

"I am glad too," said Audrey. She rubbed Sasha's tummy. He put his paws in the air. "I wish I had told the truth at the very beginning. I do not mind being clumsy sometimes. But I do not like being a liar."

"Was your project good?" asked Sara.

"I will show you," said Audrey. Audrey collected her drawings. She put them on the coffee table next to her glass of juice.

Then she held up the first drawing and stood in front of Sara.

"My book was called *Sarah, Plain and Tall,*" she said. Audrey told Sara the story and explained each picture.

When she was done, Sara clapped. "That was neat," she said. "I would like to read that book. I will ask Mommy to take me to the library."

Audrey threw out her arms in a sweeping bow. She knocked over her juice glass. Juice spilled all over her drawings.

"Oops!" said Sara.

"My drawings!" cried Audrey. The juice ran onto the floor and onto Sasha's head. He jumped up and ran away. Audrey looked at Sara. Sara was pressing her lips together, trying not to giggle.

Audrey started laughing. Sara laughed too. Then they ran to find some paper towels.

"When I left camp, Debbie was still mad at me," said Audrey. She blotted juice off of a drawing.

"I have been thinking about Debbie," said Sara. "Even after what she did, I think she needs a friend."

"Yes," said Audrey. "I just wish she knew how to be a good friend — like you."

Sara smiled. "We could teach her how to be a real friend."

"Yes," said Audrey. "That is a good idea. But how?"

"Let's call her up," said Sara. "We will ask her to come play with us tomorrow. We can make a Friends Camp for her."

Laughing, Audrey gave Sara a high five. "Sara, you are brilliant," she said. Then she reached for the phone.

L. GODWIN

About the Author

ANN M. MARTIN lives in New York City and loves animals, especially cats. She has two cats of her own, Gussie and Woody.

Other books by Ann M. Martin that you might enjoy are *Stage Fright; Me and Katie (the Pest)*; and the books in *The Baby-sitters Club* series.

Ann likes ice cream and *I Love Lucy*. And she has her own little sister, whose name is Jane.

THE KIDS IN MS. COLMAN'S CLASS

by Ann M. Martin

Don't miss #9
HALLOWEEN PARADE

Hannie began counting the squares on the calendar. "Eighteen days until Halloween," she announced. "And sixteen days until the parade."

"Sixteen days until we win prizes?" cried Chris.

"Hannie, thank you for getting our costumes," said Sara.

"This is going to be the best Halloween ever, thanks to Hannie," said Audrey.

A World of Dazzling Magi.

THE JEWEL KINGDOM

Demetra's magic mirror shows...danger!

Sparkle Mountain has caved in on the Lavendar goblins, trapping them inside the crystal mine! The Diamond Princess rushes to help — but will an angry polar bear ruin her rescue mission?

Comes with a sparkling diamor jewel necklace

THE JEWEL KINGDOM #4
The Diamond Princess Saves the Day

Jahnna N. Malcolm

Look for Jewel Kingdom books in your bookstore...and let the magic begin!